Easter Eggs-Travaganza

by Jenne Simon

SCHOLASTIC INC.

ISBN 978-0-545-60802-2

12 11 10 9 8 7 6 5 4 3 2 1
Printed in the U.S.A.

14 15 16 17 18 19/0
40

Designed by Angela Jun
First printing, January 2014

It was Easter in Lalaloopsy Land, and the sun shone down on a morning tea party.

Cotton Hoppalong was in the mood to celebrate. "I want to do something special for Easter," she told her friends.

3

"**W**e could make Easter baskets," suggested Sprouts Sunshine.
"Or decorate Easter eggs," added Alice in Lalaloopsyland.

"That sounds fun!" said Cotton. "But I'd also love to do something a little different this year...."

Peanut Big Top had an idea. "I know what to do! We can make special Easter hats. Then we can step right up and show all our friends our Easter best!"

"Easter hats!" Cotton said. "That's perfect. We can make today official Decoration Day!"

"Let's invite our friends to come over and join us," said Sprouts.

Everyone gathered at Cotton's house for the decorating party. Each friend had brought something special to decorate with.

There were jewels, markers, glitter, paper, and paint. Plus hats, eggs, and baskets, of course!

Suddenly, Cotton had an idea for all of the beautiful hats, baskets, and eggs she knew her friends would decorate. And it was a surprise she knew they'd love!

9

Jewel Sparkles grabbed some gems and got to work. She sprinkled glitter all over her hat and added jewels to the brim. It was a sparkly sensation!

Pix E. Flutters lined her hat and Easter basket with glittery ribbons. "This will protect my eggs from cracking," she said. "And it'll look gorgeous, too!"

ot Starlight picked a midnight blue hat from the pile. She sewed shiny stars onto it. Soon it looked like the night sky.

Blooms of flowers covered every square inch of Blossom Flowerpot's hat. It was alive with color, and its perfume smelled divine.

When she had enough eggs, Cotton put on her own hat. "A hippity-hoppity hat is just what I need!" she said. "Now I have to finish my secret project before anyone notices their eggs are missing. . . ."

When the decorating was done, everyone wore a picture-perfect hat and carried a matching Easter basket. Then all the girls noticed there were eggs missing.

"Where is Cotton?" asked Alice.

Cotton called to her friends from the garden. "I have a surprise for you all," she said. "I've set up an Easter egg hunt all over Lalaloopsy Land."

17

oon the Easter egg hunt had begun! It didn't take long for Jewel to spot something sparkling near Bea's house.

Blossom and Sprouts hunted for eggs in the park.
"I found one," cried Blossom.
"Me, too," said Sprouts. "Let's keep looking for more!"

19

Pix E. and Dot found eggs high and low. Peanut and Spot put on a show.

All the friends searched until they had found every last egg Cotton had hidden.

"I can't remember the last time I had so much fun on Easter," Spot exclaimed.

"I can't remember the last time we all looked so fantastically festive!" said Peanut.

When all her friends' Easter baskets were full, Cotton reappeared. "Looks like this egg hunt was a sweet success!" she said. "Now it's time for our reward. Let's eat!"

23

otton looked around her. The Easter celebration had been full of favorite activities, sweet treats, and best of all . . . fun friends! "Happy Easter, everyone!"